This Book Belongs to

Lauren

© 1985 Ron Kimball

Sophie's Surprise

Shirley Holt & Lee Richardson

ShirLee

Dedicated to:
Our Children

A Special Thanks To:
Pomper

Andrea

Muschka

Ryan

Frieda

La Verta

Doc

Second Edition 1984
First Edition 1983
Text Copyright © 1983 by Lee Richardson
Illustrations Copyright © 1983 by Shirley Holt
All rights reserved under International and Pan-American Copyright Convention. Printed in the
United States by Herald Printers for ShirLee Publications, Post Office Box 22122,
Carmel, California 93922.
ISBN 0-9613476-0-0

Mr. Kelly found Sophie in the alley

behind his toy store.

She was hungry and needed a home.

He was lonely and needed a mouser.

"Poor cat," said Mr. Kelly.
"I will feed you.
You can live in my toy store."

"Meow," said Sophie.
"I will catch mice."

"We will work together, Sophie.
During the day it is my job to sell toys.
When night comes, it will be your job
to hunt for mice."

"Meow, I will work hard," she said.

Mr. Kelly put on his coat and hat.
"Good night, Sophie.
It is time for me to go home."
He reached in his pocket for the key
and locked the toy store door.
"Good hunting!" he called.

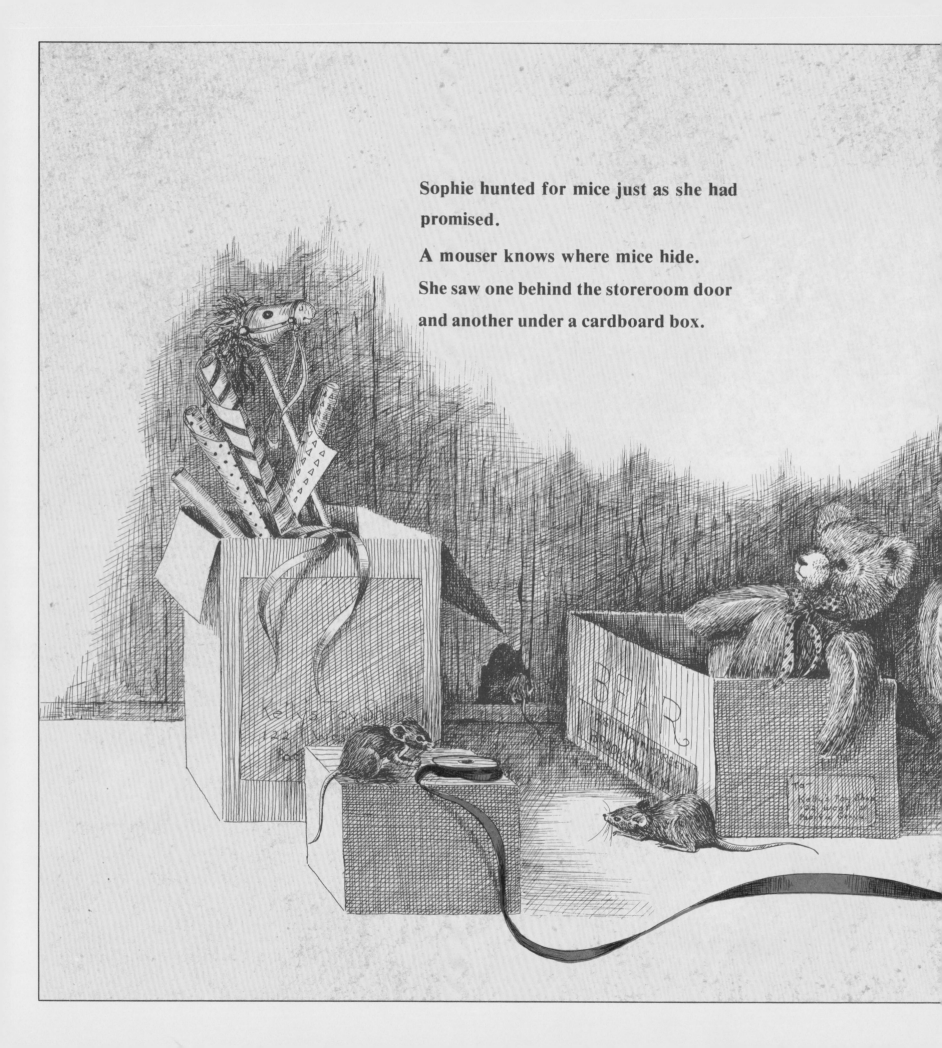

Sophie hunted for mice just as she had
promised.

A mouser knows where mice hide.
She saw one behind the storeroom door
and another under a cardboard box.

Once she saw three!

They were squeaking with delight, nibbling on crumbs from Mr. Kelly's lunch.

The mice looked up. They saw Sophie!

Sophie leaped, but they scurried away and disappeared through a hole in the wall.

Sophie's job was over for this night.

The sun was coming up.

She washed her face and listened for the sound

of the bell over the toy store door.

It rang every time the door was opened.

"Ting-a-ling!

Ting-a-ling!"

"Good morning, Sophie," called Mr. Kelly.

"How is my store detective?"

"Meow, I am hungry.

Hunting for mice is hard work."

He poured milk into a bowl.

"Here is your breakfast, Sophie."

She lapped up the milk and licked the sides

of the bowl.

Then she looked for a place to sleep.

Sophie tried sleeping many places. But none felt right.

She leaped high on a shelf and found a big brown bear.

She stepped round and round, sniffing his ears and nose.

Brown Bear did not move or make noise.

His fur felt soft and warm. So she curled up in his lap.
Sophie had found the best place to sleep.

"Tap, tap, tap," went Mr. Kelly's hammer.

He hung holly and pine boughs all over the toy store.

Sophie yawned.

"How can I sleep with all this noise? Meow!"

"Ah, sleepy head, there is work to be done.

Soon it will be Christmas.

I must decorate the toy store and put a tree in the window."

"Meow, I will help you," said Sophie.

Instead she closed her eyes.   She slept all afternoon.

Every afternoon until Christmas, Sophie slept while Mr. Kelly was busy selling toys.

He wrapped them in red and green paper for every customer.

He unpacked boxes and stacked more toys on the shelves.

"Selling toys is hard work," he said to himself.

"I need help. Where is my helper?

Ah, Sophie, you have slept long enough. Wake up!"

"Wake up, Sophie!" called Mr. Kelly.

"I want to put Brown Bear in the window.

Maybe someone will buy him.

He needs a home too!"

Sophie opened her eyes.

"Tomorrow is Christmas Day," he said.

"Brown Bear will make some little child happy."

"Meow! He makes me happy now!" said

Sophie, arching her back.

"I love Brown Bear.

I will growl and show my teeth if anyone tries to buy him!"

Mr. Kelly did not hear her.

He put Brown Bear in the window where everyone could

see him.

"Ting-a-ling!
Ting-a-ling!"
Christmas shoppers kept opening and closing
the toy store door.
"Ting-a-ling!
Ting-a-ling!"
Mr. Kelly sold toys until the moon came up!

At last the bell was quiet.
It was seven o'clock.
It was time to lock the door and go home.

"Sophie?

Sophie?" called Mr. Kelly.

She did not answer.

"Sophie, tonight you will not hunt for mice.

You will come home with me.

We will spend Christmas Eve together.

Sophie?"

Then he remembered he had not seen her for several hours.

He looked under the table.

She was not there.

He looked inside boxes and high on the shelves.

He could not find her.

"Sophie?

Sophie?"

Suddenly Mr. Kelly heard laughter.

He was surprised to see people standing in front of the toy store.

Children pressed their noses to the windowpane.

Some were pointing, and everyone was laughing.

He hurried to see.

He laughed too!

Five tiny kittens, their eyes tightly closed, were
nestled in Brown Bear's fur.
"Sophie!" Mr. Kelly exclaimed.
"Sophie, you have given us a special gift.
Five little mousers!"
He stroked her head gently.
"You and your family will come home with me."

Mr. Kelly went to get a basket to hold Sophie
and her babies.
Sophie watched as he lifted her kittens carefully
into the basket.
"Come along, Sophie. We are going home.
Jump into the basket," he said. "Come along!"
Sophie did not move.

Mr. Kelly smiled.

"All right, Sophie. All right," he said.

"Brown Bear will come home with us too."